INDOOR SUPER SKILLS!

TO ______________________

FOLLOW YOUR DREAMS!

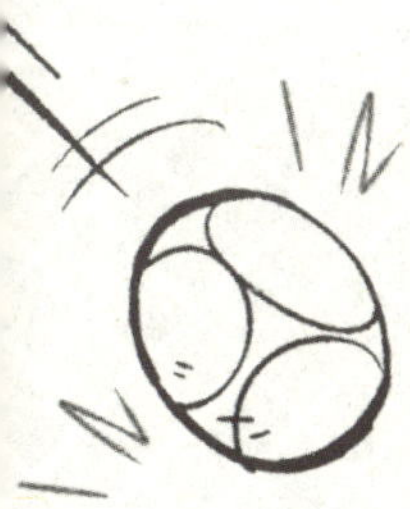

A Scholastic Australia Book

Scholastic Australia
An imprint of Scholastic Australia Pty Limited
PO Box 579 Gosford NSW 2250
ABN 11 000 614 577
www.scholastic.com.au

Part of the Scholastic Group
Sydney • Auckland • New York • Toronto • London • Mexico City
• New Delhi • Hong Kong • Buenos Aires • Puerto Rico

Published by Scholastic Australia in 2023.

Text by Tim Cahill and Julian Gray.

Illustrations by Heath McKenzie.

A catalogue record for this book is available from the National Library of Australia

Typeset in Mozzart Sketch and Bizzle Chizzle.

Printed in China by Hang Tai Printing Company Limited.
This product is made of material from well-managed FSC®-certified forests, recycled materials, and other controlled sources.

24 25 26 27 28 / 2

CHAPTER 1

'Alright, everyone, let's **hurry up and get going**!' I said.

'To school?' said Shae. **'What's the rush?!'**

Shae was right—I wasn't always this excited to get to school. Especially when it was the first day of a new term, like today was. But **this day was different**!

You see, our friend Nic from Sunshine Island had come to visit. And not only that, he was staying with

us and was going to be joining our class at school for a whole term—as well as **playing on our soccer team**, the **LIONS**!

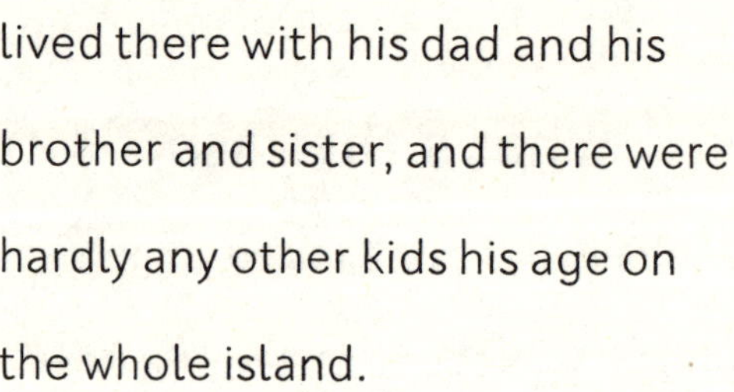

Nic and I really hit it off when our family went to Sunshine Island for a holiday. He lived there with his dad and his brother and sister, and there were hardly any other kids his age on the whole island.

There weren't enough kids for a soccer league—there weren't even enough kids for one team!

Nic had actually never seen a full-size, proper grass pitch before—he'd only ever **played on the sand**!

Still, I had been **blown away** by how good his soccer skills were! We'd had some amazing games of beach soccer when our family visited. In fact, we'd had

The Most <u>Epic</u> Beach Soccer Game Ever–

or at least, that's what we called it!

And now, I couldn't wait to get to school early so I could show Nic our oval and have a kick around with my friends before class started. I was sure **he was going to be super impressed**!

We each grabbed a piece of fruit and ran out the door. This was **going to be a fun day**!

We met Mike at the corner. As we walked to school, Nic had a bunch of questions. We'd picked him up from the airport only yesterday, and there were **a lot of things that were new to him**!

'Are there always this many cars around?' he asked.

'No,' I said. 'There's **usually heaps more** traffic than this.'

Nic looked shocked! 'Woah,' he said. 'I've never seen roads this busy!'

'You should see it at peak time, when everyone drives to work and school,' said Mike.

Nic shook his head, and asked, 'Well, are there always this many people around?'

'This is nothing!' said Shae. There were a few kids walking to school, some grown-ups waiting at the bus stop, and some people jogging or walking to the shops.

'I guess it's going to **take some getting used to**,' Nic said.

We nodded.

'Just like I'll have to get used to **all the noise, all the time**,' Nic added.

'What do you mean?' asked Shae. 'It isn't noisy. Is it?' Shae looked at me.

I shook my head. 'What kind of noise?' I asked Nic.

'I woke up really early this morning and couldn't go back to sleep,' Nic said. 'Cars, trains, airplanes, sirens–'

'Mum snoring . . .' added Shae.

'Well, yes, but it was mostly outside your house,' said Nic. 'I'm used to **birds and insects and frogs**. And **only two plane trips a week**, one dropping off a load of visitors and one taking another load home.'

'You'll be used to it before you know it,' I said. 'You won't even notice it in a few days.'

Nic shrugged.

We were nearly at school. And just around the corner was the oval where our soccer pitch was. I was **so excited to introduce Nic** to the rest of my friends, who we'd arranged to meet–and to start kicking the ball around.

I knew everyone would think his **skills were top-level amazing**!

As we got closer and closer, I noticed a bunch of big trucks driving past. It actually was starting to get noisy! And for some reason there was a lot of **dust swirling around** in the air. I wondered what was going on . . .

And then we saw it. Our amazing oval, the place I'd been so excited to show Nic, had trucks and diggers all over it! The whole pitch was . . . **a giant heap of dirt**!

'Ta-da,' said Shae, not quite sure how to present the disaster in front of us to Nic!

Sienna, Ricardo and Millie were standing just up ahead. And like us, they looked completely shocked!

Studs and Hacker were there, too . . .

'Have you got **something to do with this**, Tiny Timmy?' asked Studs.

'Yeah, it's got **your fingerprints all over it**,' agreed Hacker.

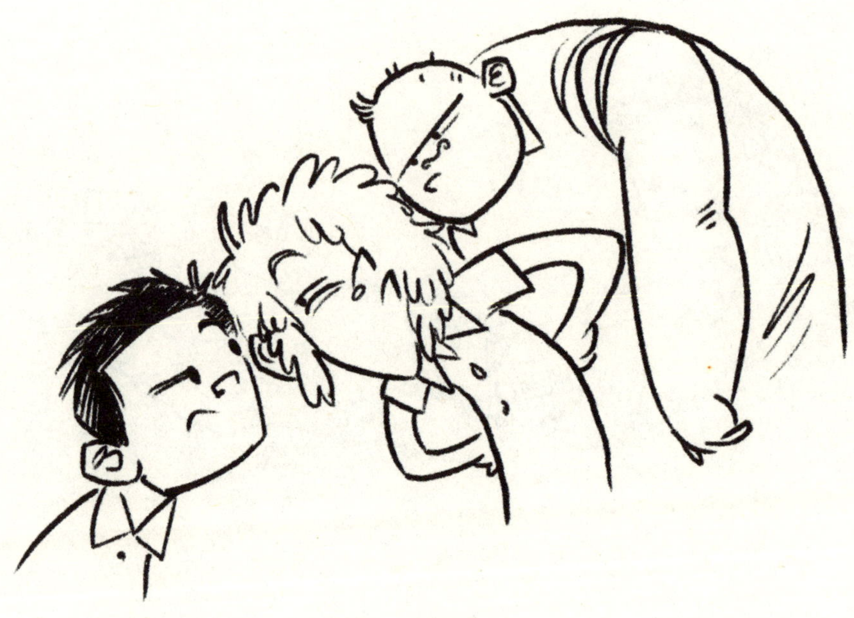

None of us had any idea what was going on, or why our beautiful oval now looked like a construction site!

I couldn't believe it! I felt a bit embarrassed in front of Nic, but he knew there was nothing I could do about it. I took the chance to introduce him to the rest of my friends. After all I'd told them about Nic, everyone was **really happy to finally meet him**.

There was only one person who might be able to tell us what was going on, and that was Coach Roach! We walked on through the school gates, **hoping to get some answers**!

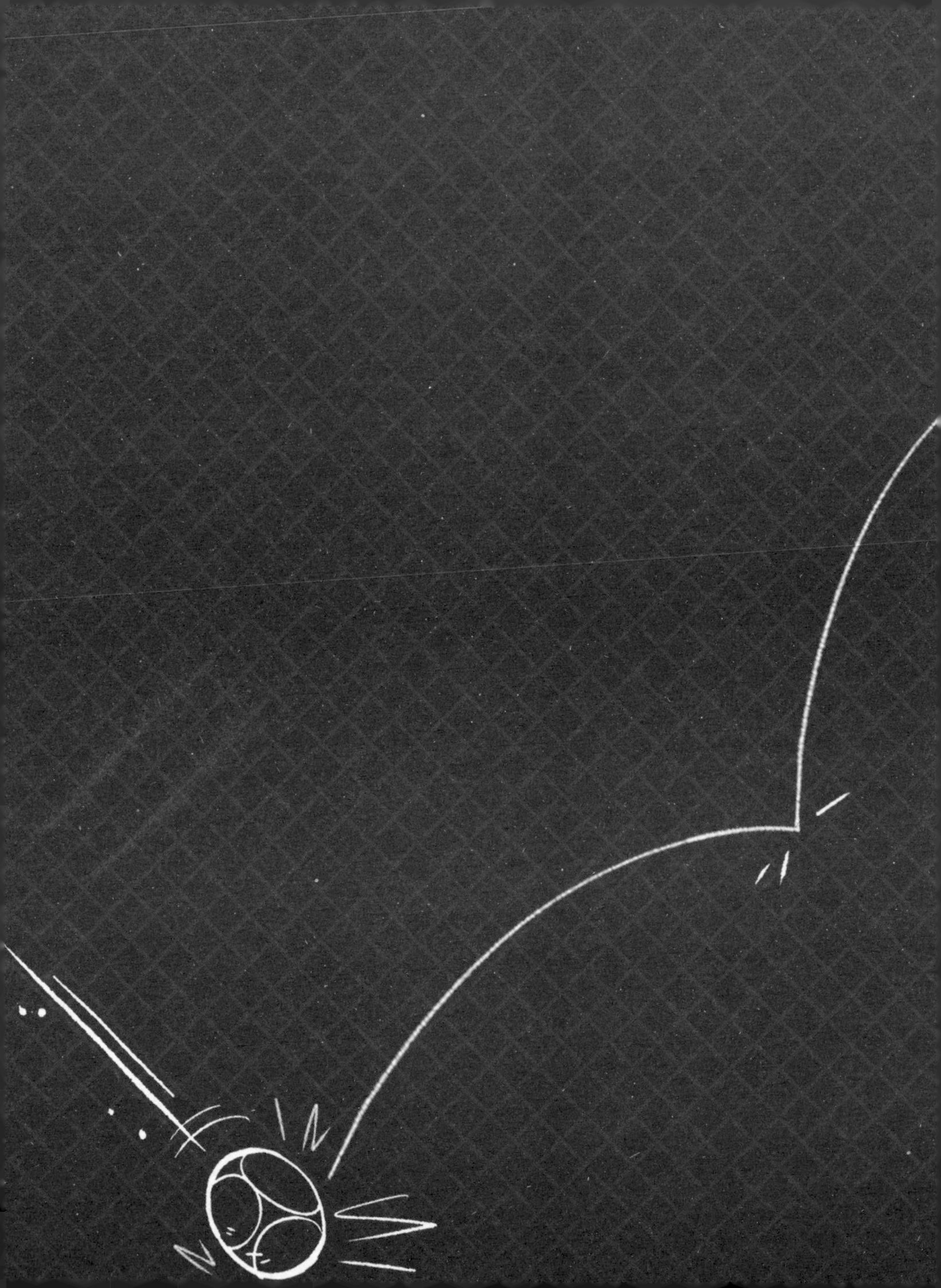

CHAPTER 2

'Did I not tell you all about this?' asked Coach Roach, once we'd got to class.

'Um, no, Coach—you left out the part about how **our soccer pitch was getting dug up**, right in the middle of the season,' I said.

'Oh, sorry about that,' said Coach. 'Anyway, it's **absolutely fantastic news**!'

We all looked at each other.

'Whaaaaaaat?!' I eventually said.

'How can this be good news?!'

'Well,' Coach said, 'the pitch isn't going to look like that forever. It's getting returfed!'

'Which means . . . what, exactly?' asked Mike.

'It means that new grass is going to be laid,' said Coach Roach. 'It's **going to look absolutely amazing**! Like a pitch the professionals would play on—covered in perfect grass!'

'Oh, great!' I said. 'When will we be able to play on it again? **Tomorrow?**'

'Not quite,' laughed Coach Roach.

'No way!' I said. 'Are we going to have to wait until **the weekend**?'

'Wrong again,' said Coach. 'There's going to be **weeks of waiting** until we can play on our home pitch again.'

'Whaaaaaat?!'

we all shouted.

'I'm afraid so,' Coach said. 'They have to finish digging up the ground, then lay the new grass down, water it, and get it growing. Only then will we be allowed back on to play.'

'This. Is. A. Disaster.' I said, throwing my hands up in the air.

'Maybe for some,' said Studs. 'But not for Hacker and I, oh no. Coach is right, **this is going to be a very good thing**.'

'How is that possible?' asked Sienna.

'Well, you see, I've always felt this pitch has held us back. Just Hacker and I, that is–not all of you.'

'Yeah,' said Hacker. 'You lot are **as good now as you're ever going to get**.'

'Correct,' said Studs. 'But true skill players, like Hacker and I, have been brought back to your level by the substandard surface on which we've been playing. A new pitch will allow us to, what's the word . . .'

'Flourish,' said Hacker.

'Exactly!' said Studs. He gave Hacker a high five.

We all rolled our eyes.

'But Coach,' I said, '**this is a big problem**! Where are we going to play our games?'

'We'll be playing our games away from home for the next few weeks,' Coach said. 'Then, when our new pitch is ready, we'll have a lot of home games to make up for it.'

'OK,' Mike said, 'but where are we going to train? We're in the middle of our season, **we can't just stop training**.'

'That's where it gets a little bit . . . complicated,' said Coach Roach.

'What does that mean?!' I asked.

'Well, training is going to be a bit different for the next few weeks,' Coach said. 'We're going to be training inside. In the school hall. On the basketball court.'

'Whaaaaaat?!' we all said. It was the first of a lot more questions!

'The basketball court is so small! How will we play practice games?'

'And it doesn't have proper full-size goals! How can we have shooting practice?'

'How can the keeper practise kick-outs? And how will we play long balls?'

'What are we going to do for corner-kick practice? There's not enough room!'

'We won't be able to wear our boots on the wooden floor! What shoes will we wear?'

I was not sure this was a great idea!

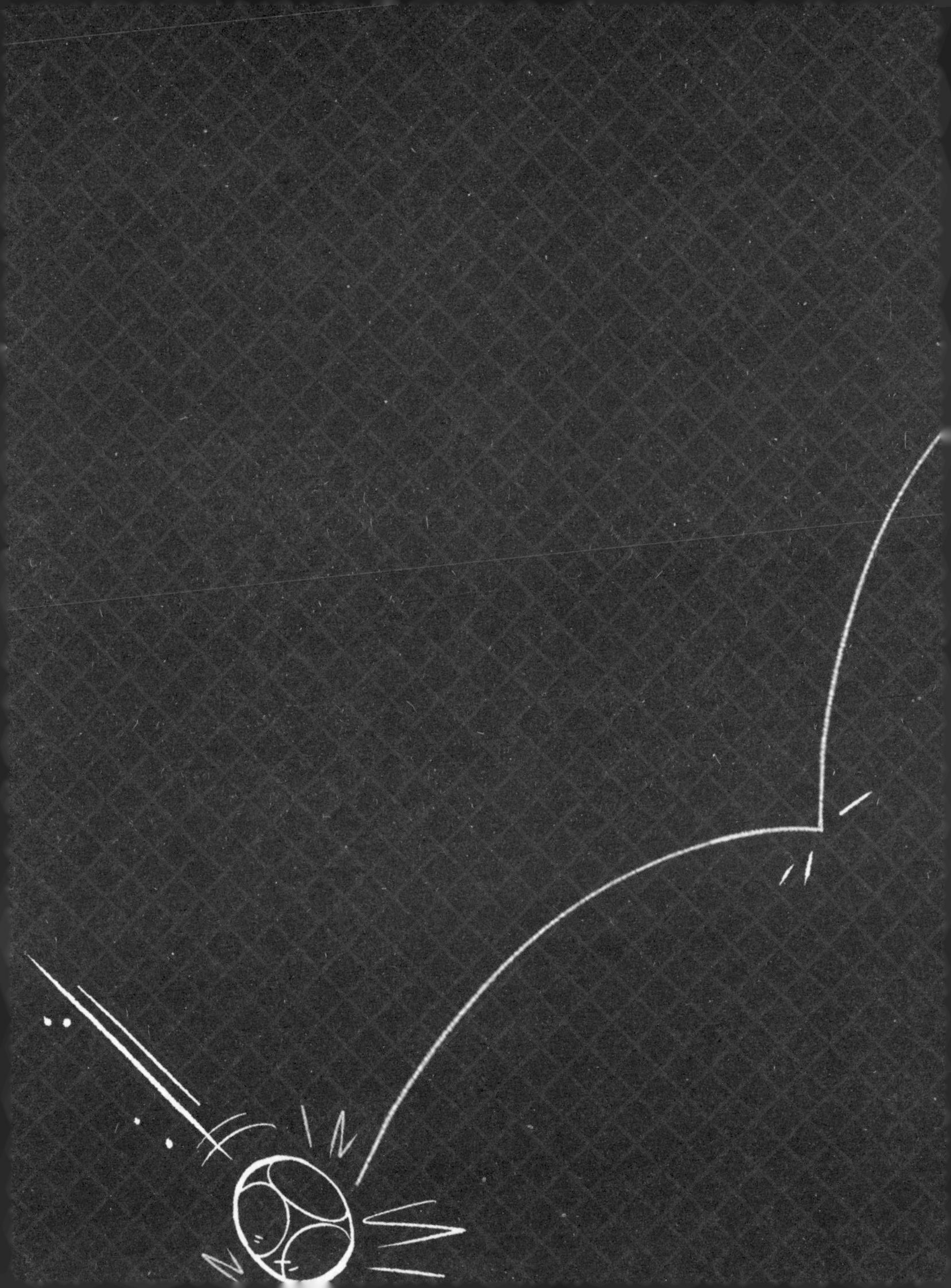

CHAPTER 3

For the rest of the day, we tried to help Nic get used to life at our school.

His entire school on Sunshine Island had the same amount of kids as there were just in our class. It was no wonder that it was all a bit overwhelming for him!

We had an assembly where the principal spoke to all the kids. I don't think Nic had ever seen **so many people in the same place** at once!

And I know he thought it was crazy at lunchtime when **everyone was running around** playing soccer, tag, handball and hopscotch! He got used to it pretty soon, though, and before long everyone could see what I'd been telling them about his soccer skills was true.

When the bell rang for the end of school, we all headed to the hall for our first training session. And it was . . . **absolute craziness**!

We were all running around without much idea of what we were supposed to be doing, with soccer balls **bouncing all over the place**. And that was problem number one!

The balls that Coach Roach had brought to training were the same balls we played with all the time.

That was fine when we were playing outside on grass, but inside on the hard floor they were **waaaaay too bouncy**! They kept bouncing over our heads, and were impossible to control!

The next problem was our shoes. At our normal outdoor training sessions we'd all be wearing our boots, but here in the hall **everyone had different sneakers**. Some of us had shoes that were too slippery, some were too grippy—and even though I'd brought an extra pair for Nic, he chose to go barefoot!

Then there was the problem for our goalkeeper, Liam. He was expected to dive around everywhere making saves on the hard, wooden floor. And all of the shots on goal were coming from really close—which **looked super painful**!

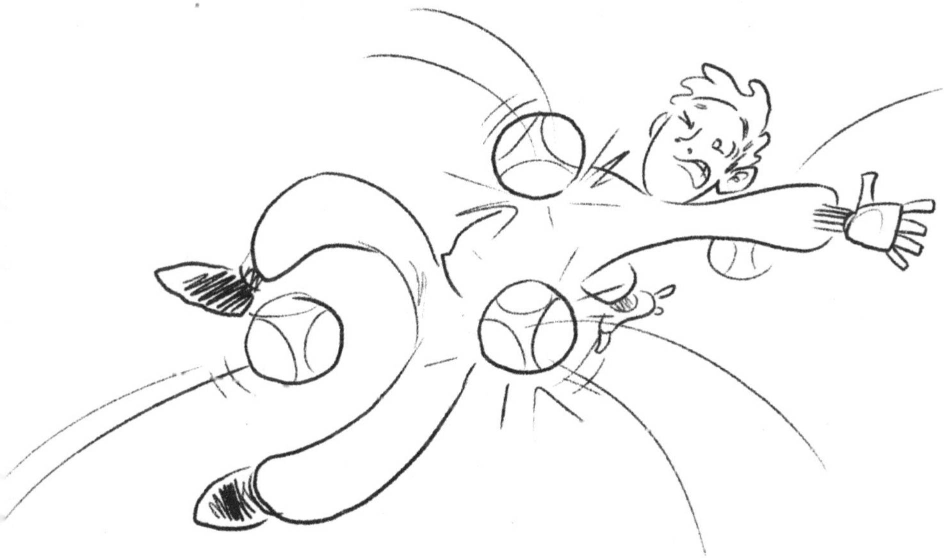

I was just glad that I was an outfield player and **didn't have to go in goal**!

A big problem that we all had, though, was . . .

Hacker and Studs.

It was one thing to be slide tackled outside on the grass. It was another thing to be slide tackled inside, on the hard floor! Studs and Hacker were **flying in with crazy tackles**, even though it must have been hurting them as much as it was hurting us!

I was dribbling the ball slowly, looking to play a pass, when **Hacker ➡ launched himself** and took the ball, and my legs, out from under me.

Ouch! I hit the floor with a huge thud. I was definitely going to have some big bruises tomorrow!

Eventually Coach Roach had to stop the session and tell Hacker and Studs that **slide tackles were not allowed** in indoor soccer.

'What do you mean, Coach?!' said Studs. 'How are we supposed to make a tackle if we can't come leaping in with absolutely no control of our own bodies or what's going to happen to the ball carrier?'

'Yeah,' said Hacker. 'It's pretty much top of our skill set.'

'Ever heard of staying on your feet and taking the ball in a clean tackle?' asked Sienna.

'No,' said Studs and Hacker.

Studs went on, **'Perhaps you'd like to hear our motto?'**

Nobody did, but that didn't stop Studs.

'Ready, Hack? Let's give it to them.'

'If you don't end up on the ground, **your tackle technique isn't sound**,' recited Hacker and Studs in unison.

We all started to groan, but Studs cut us off.

'Wait, we're not done,' Studs said. He looked at Hacker and they went on.

'It's not a proper tackle, if you don't hear joints crackle,' they said, and gave each other another big high five.

'Wow,' I said. 'How long did it take you to come up with that?'

'Just a couple of weeks,' said Studs.

We all shook our heads, while Coach Roach reminded everyone–well, Hacker and Studs–that slide tackles were **definitely against the rules**.

The thing was, there was actually no need for slide tackles. As soon as anyone took one bad touch, whoever was marking them found it easy to take the ball away.

And that was the biggest problem of all–it was just **such a small space to be practising in**!

It wasn't like outdoor soccer where Mike or Sienna could go for a great, long run down the sideline to get past defenders. And you couldn't play a really long ball to cut out a bunch of players, either.

To get past defenders and make our way down the court, we had to play a lot of quick, short passes, and **every touch had to be perfect**! Plus, because everyone was so close, we had to always be checking around to keep an eye on where the defenders were!

The only one of us who knew what they were doing was Sienna. Whenever she got the ball she took a touch or two, passed it and moved into space.

If we could all do that, **we'd definitely be onto something**!

Sienna said **she'd played indoor soccer before**, and that's how she'd learnt a lot of the important skills. She said she even had a pair of proper indoor boots that she'd make sure to bring to training next time!

We were all kind of relieved when Coach Roach blew the whistle for the end of the session. **It had been hard work**, and we all had the bumps and burns from sliding on the wood floor to show for it!

I was sorry that Nic hadn't been able to play on our big grass pitch, but he didn't seem to mind. It looked like it was something **we'd all have to get used to**, anyway . . .

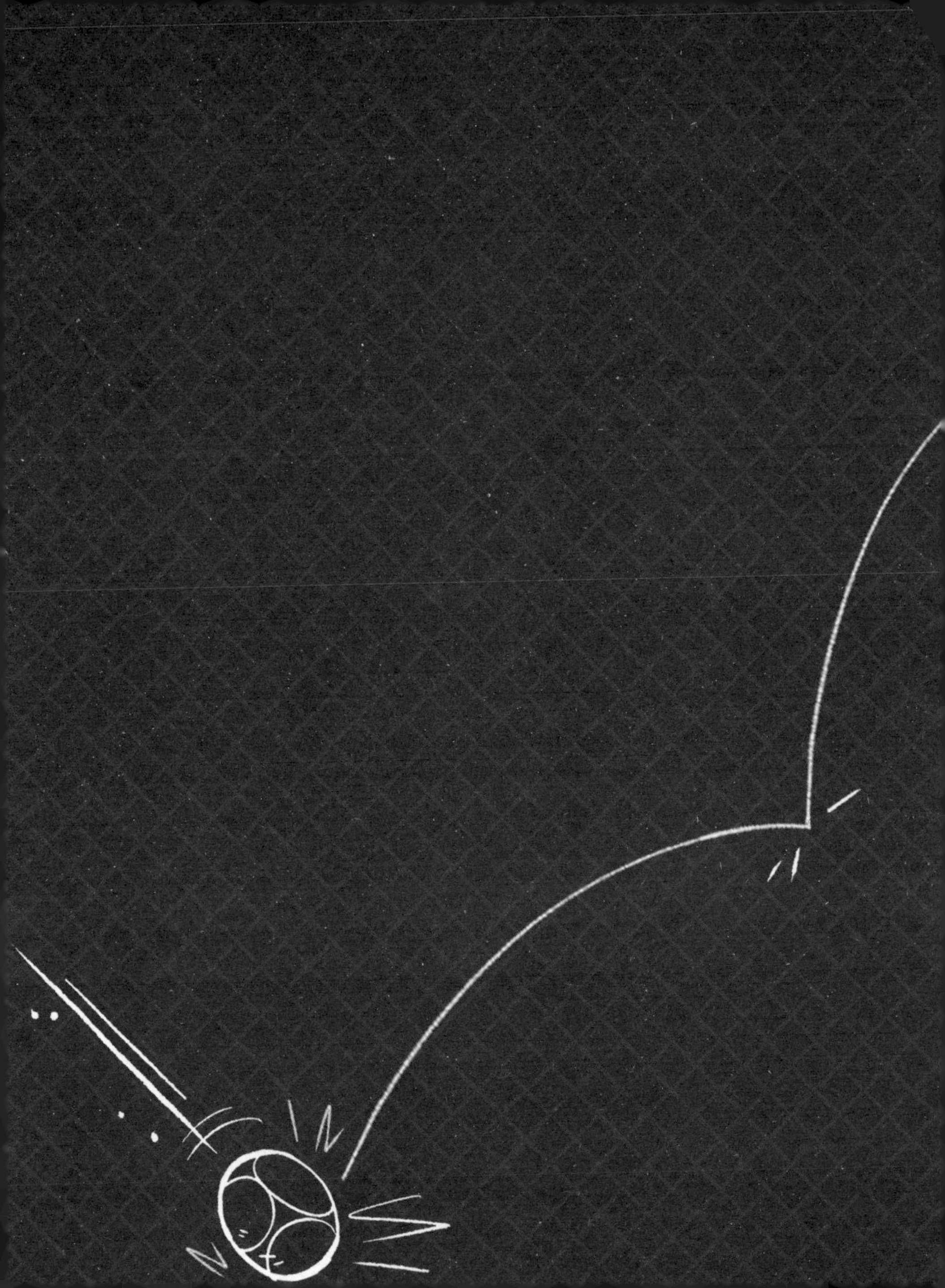

CHAPTER 4

When I woke up the next morning and took a few steps, **I was . . . sore**.

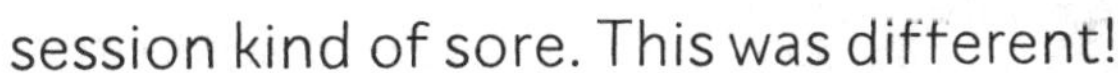
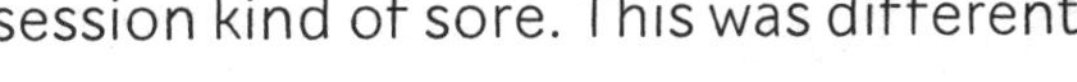
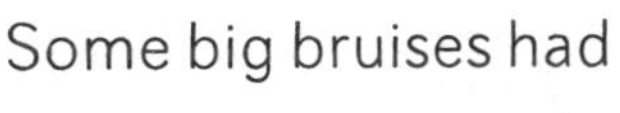

And not the regular, just-had-a-serious-training-session kind of sore. This was different! Some big bruises had come up from when I'd hit the hard floor after being tackled.

And I had **a bunch of burns** on my legs and arms from when I'd slid across the wood. Ouch!

Nic had some bumps and bruises too—he'd never got those from playing in the sand at home! I was sure he'd been wondering what he'd got himself into!

All day at school we walked around super slowly, **wincing after what seemed like every step**! Thankfully, by the time the bell rang at the end of the day we were just about used to our injuries.

And ready to get some more . . . because it was time for our next training session!

As we walked into the hall, Studs and Hacker were already there talking to Coach Roach. They looked up as they saw us come in.

‘Well, would you **take a look at this lot**,’ said Studs. ‘Hobbling around like they’ve never had a training session before!’

‘We wouldn’t have as many bumps if it weren’t for you guys and your crazy slide tackles,’ I said. ‘Anyway, what are you doing here? You’re never early for training.’

‘As a matter of fact,’ said Studs, ‘we were here to have a word to Coach about the “no-slide-tackle” rule. Our feeling is that it **unfairly affects myself and Hacker**.’

'Yeah,' agreed Hacker. 'In what kind of world are you not allowed to make **good, clean tackles**?'

'As I've explained, lads,' said Coach Roach, 'slide tackles are against the rules in indoor soccer for a good reason—the floor is much harder than grass, and the risk of injury is too high.'

'If you say so, Coach,' said Studs. **'But I don't like it.'** He and Hacker both gave a thumbs-down sign.

'We're all going to have to get used to training here in the hall,' said Coach. 'Because it's not going to change until the school oval is ready for us to play on again.'

We all groaned.

'It's not so bad, is it?' asked Coach. 'We still need to stay sharp for our matches, and this is the best way to keep in good nick. You might even find that the skills we work on in here will **help you get a lot better** at outdoor soccer.'

Sienna was nodding along. 'It's true,' she said. 'Playing on the small pitch really helps to **get your technique right**–if you take a bad touch, you lose the ball.'

We'd all found that out at yesterday's session!

'Plus,' Sienna went on, 'so many of the top players around the world grew up playing indoor soccer–it's **where they got their super skills** from!'

'I've heard that, too,' said Mike. 'And the **proper name for indoor soccer is "futsal"**, right Coach?'

'Foot sole?' said Studs. 'We're just making stuff up now, are we? In that case, why don't we call it **"indoorsy kicky-wicky"**?'

'Yeah,' said Hacker, 'or how about "big waste of time because we're not allowed to make perfectly legitimate slide tackles or even boot the ball down the other end"?'

'Wow, that last one **really rolls off the tongue**,' I said with a smile.

'Not "foot sole",' said Coach Roach. 'It's futsal, which comes from Spanish and Portuguese, and means "hall football". And that's exactly what we're doing– **playing football in the hall**!'

'Makes sense to me!' I said.

'And to make it easier to play football in the hall,' Coach said, 'I've brought some real futsal balls along for us to train with.'

'Hooray!' I said. 'But wait–how are they different to outdoor balls?'

Sienna knew the answer. 'They're a bit smaller, they're heavier and they don't bounce as much.' She kicked a ball over to me. **It was much easier to control!**

So that was one big problem solved–we wouldn't have soccer balls bouncing all around our heads, and we wouldn't be so likely to lose the ball after every single touch we took! **Things were looking better already!**

'The balls aren't all,' said Coach Roach, walking over to the kit bag. He opened it up, and said, 'Futsal shoes for everyone!'

Now this was a game changer!

They were only on loan to us, and not everyone got exactly the right size, but having proper shoes made a huuuuge difference! No more slipping, no more sticking! Now two of our big problems had been fixed, just by **having the right equipment**!

Next up Coach Roach had some practice drills for us to do. Now that we knew we'd be training in the hall until our outdoor pitch was ready again, we were happy our sessions were going to be more organised than the **out-of-control craziness** of yesterday!

The drills were to help us get used to playing in tight spaces. The first one was pretty simple– everyone took a turn at running down the court, **weaving in and out** of cones while dribbling the ball.

Most of us didn't have too much of a problem with this drill. The key was making sure the ball didn't get too far away from you on the hard–and quick–surface!

Nic did a great job, especially since the surface he was used to dribbling on was sand! I was **really happy he was fitting in** so well with the team!

Not everyone did quite as well as Nic, though.

Studs had to keep doubling back to get through the cones, because he'd kicked the ball too far to weave his way smoothly through. But at least he did make it through all the cones . . .

Hacker just **booted the ball** down the other end of the court with one kick, then ran straight through all the cones, knocking them over as he went by.

'Hmm, just a bit strong there, Hack,' said Studs.

Hacker didn't seem too worried. '***Fastest* time yet**, right Coach?' he asked.

‘Well, yes, it was fast,’ Coach Roach said. ‘But maybe next time you could include some dribbling and weaving through the cones?’

‘Don’t think so, Coach,’ said Hacker. **‘That’d just slow me down.’**

I don’t think Hacker understood just what we were trying to achieve with this drill!

Coach Roach called the next drill 'boxed in'. He put four cones in a square, each side about two metres long. We all took turns standing inside the square, while someone kicked the ball towards us.

We had to control the ball without it going outside the square. It was a really good exercise because it made us concentrate on our technique in **keeping the ball in a small space**.

Perfect skills for futsal!

After a few turns each, we all got better at it– even when the ball came in at chest–or even head–height!

But again, Hacker didn't quite get it–each time the ball came to him in the square, he just **took a big swing at it**, aiming for distance each time.

'Woah, did you see that one?' he called, after smashing another one away. '**Nearly broke a window** at the back of the hall!'

After that, Coach Roach moved on to some different drills . . . and we all felt like we were **starting to get the hang of things in the hall**. Well, everyone except for Studs and Hacker, who continued to run into the wrong spaces and loudly complain about how small the court was.

'If you can control the ball in this tight space,' Coach Roach said, 'and learn to pass and move quickly, **it will make playing outside seem easy** when you have so much more space to work with.'

'Sounds great to me!' I said, and my friends all agreed.

'Excellent!' said Coach Roach. 'Now, who's ready for our first five-a-side futsal game?'

We all put up our hands. **Bring it on!**

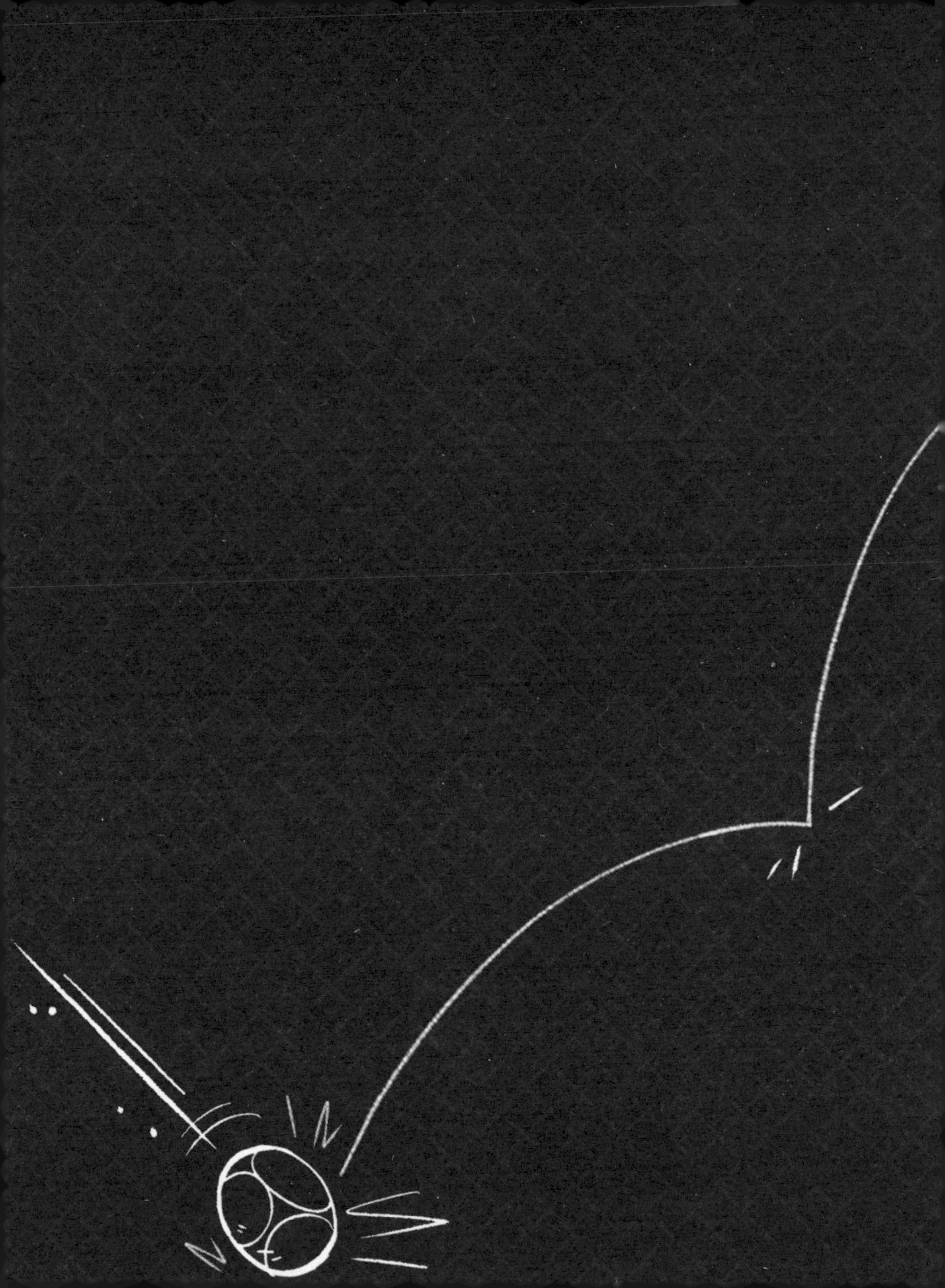

CHAPTER 5

The good news was we were finally going to play a game, and Nic and Ricardo were on my team! The not-quite-so-good news was that Hacker and Studs were also on our team—so we weren't exactly sure how that was going to go!

The even worse news was that Liam—our goalkeeper—was on the other team. Which meant that we'd all have to **take turns being in goal**! Uh-oh!

Studs and Hacker weren't worried about any of it.

'Have no fear, Tiny Timmy and friends,' said Studs. '**We'll win this game, easy.** We won't even have to raise a sweat.'

'Yeah,' said Hacker. 'I predict we'll win eight-, maybe ten-nil.'

'As long as you all **don't do anything silly**,' added Studs. 'Anyway, I'm just glad those ridiculous drills are over and done with—we've been waiting to play a game this whole time.'

I was pretty sure Nic, Ricardo and I weren't going to do anything silly . . . I just hoped we'd be able to make up for **whatever Studs and Hacker were about to do**!

Before we started our game, Coach Roach explained some more of the rules.

'When the ball goes over the sideline, there are no throw-ins. Instead, you'll kick the ball in from where it went out,' Coach said.

We all nodded.

'Next,' Coach went on, 'there are no goal kicks. When the ball goes over the goal lines at the ends of the court, the keeper throws it out.'

We nodded again.

'And lastly,' Coach continued, '**there are no offsides in futsal**.'

We nodded—but I could also see Studs and Hacker's eyes light up. And then give each other a big, excited high five! I knew this was

not going to be good for us!

But first, **we needed a goalkeeper**. I asked everyone who wanted to go in goal for the first few minutes of the game.

As soon as I'd finished asking the question, Studs and Hacker froze. Is was like they'd turned into statues.

'Did you hear what I said?' I asked them.

They both stayed perfectly still. **I poked Studs in the arm, then Hacker.** Nothing!

'Really, you guys?!' I said. 'I know you can hear me!'

'Looks like they definitely don't want to be in goal,' said Ricardo. 'I don't know how I'll go, but I'll take the first shift.'

The rest of us thanked Ricardo as he jogged off into our goal, while Studs and Hacker **magically came back to life**.

The opposition kicked off–and **they looked amazing**! Their team included Sienna, Mike and Millie, and they moved the ball around super quickly, just playing a touch or two and then running into space.

Our team, on the other hand, **wasn't looking quite so good** . . .

From the kick-off, Hacker and Studs ran up and plonked themselves right in front of Liam in the other team's goal. Which meant me and Nic were left to run around all over the place, chasing the ball and trying to **defend four players all on our own**!

Whenever we did manage to win the ball back, Studs and Hacker started waving their arms and calling for us to pass to them, shouting, 'Strikers in the clear!'

I asked Coach Roach for a quick time out.

'What are you doing up there?' I said to Hacker and Studs.

'Tiny Timmy, I don't know if you heard what Coach said, but there are no offsides,' said Studs. 'Which means we can stand right up in front of the goal.'

'**It's like heaven** for top strikers like us,' said Hacker.

'First,' I said, 'nobody made you guys strikers. Second, I don't even think we should be playing with strikers–especially not two of you! And third–we really need you to come back and help defend!'

'I'm afraid **defending is not in the striker's job description**,' said Studs.

'Yeah, it's just not really part of how we're put together as footballers,' said Hacker.

I didn't think I was going to be able **to get through to them**.

Coach Roach blew the whistle for the game to restart. It wasn't long before **Nic and I were completely exhausted** from all the running we had to do to keep up with Sienna, Mike and Millie. We weren't going to be able to keep this up for too much longer!

Ricardo wasn't having much fun in goal, either.

Because they always had spare players in attack, the other team was able to take lots and lots of shots! And most of them had **crashed into Ricardo's body**!

I mean, technically they were saves, so Ricardo had done well. I don't think he saw it that way, though—he was too busy **counting up the bruises**!

On their next attack, Mike played a really nice one-two pass with Sienna. As the ball came back to him, Mike hit **a super-hard shot from point-blank range**, right at Ricardo.

Ricardo stuck out an arm, but we could tell he didn't really want to get behind it after all the hits he'd already taken. The ball went **smashing into the net**–one-nil to the other team!

'What do you call that?!' called Studs, from way down the other end of the court.

'Yeah,' said Hacker. 'The goalkeeper really has to do better there.'

'Well, it's time for us to change keepers,' I said. 'Perhaps one of you could take a turn?'

And with that, **Studs and Hacker completely froze again**.

'Alright you guys, you can't just bring out the old "we've turned into statues" routine every time someone asks you to be goalkeeper!' I said. **'We all have to take a turn!'**

Studs and Hacker stayed frozen.

I shook my head.

Nic said, 'It's OK, I'll have a turn in goal.'

'Are you sure?' I asked. 'Looks like **it can get pretty rough in there**!'

Nic was happy to give it a go, so Ricardo and I went up to take the kick-off. As soon as we did, Studs and Hacker jogged up in front of Liam again. It looked like Ricardo and I would have to do a lot more defending!

We decided to sit back in front of Nic, and try not to use too much energy running all over the court. But with Hacker and Studs not helping to defend at all, we were still outnumbered, and before much time had passed we were **just about ready to drop**!

Ricardo and I did our best to protect our goal—and Nic—but the others were still able to get a bunch of shots away. Nic took a few hits, but was doing **a really good job** and we'd managed to keep them out!

In the middle of another one of the other team's attacks, I was able to intercept a pass before it got through to Mike. Ricardo was in a bit of space, so I passed the ball to him, **and he hit it l-o-n-g**, up towards our goal.

Studs was standing right in front of Liam, and his eyes lit up. He took a big swing, and . . . completely missed it with his kicking foot. But then he, and the rest of us, looked on in amazement as the ball rolled through, took a deflection off his standing foot, and **went into the goal**!

We'd scored, to level the game up at 1-1!

And with that, Coach Roach blew the whistle for half time. Ricardo, Nic and I went over to the sideline and **collapsed on our bench**.

Studs and Hacker strolled down from the other end of the court.

'See what happens when someone finally decides to pass us the ball?' said Studs.

'Magic is what happens,' said Hacker.

'Magic?! That was a mistake! And anyway, we weren't not passing you the ball on purpose,' I said. 'We almost never had the ball because we were **running around from one side of the court to the other** chasing it!'

'Maybe if you guys came back to defend, we'd have the ball more and could **actually do some attacking ourselves**,' added Ricardo.

'All I'll say is that we'd be winning, if only the rest of the team gave us a bit more support,' said Studs.

'Yeah,' said Hacker. **'Help us to help you.'**

These two were just unbelievable!

As the second half was about to kick off, Coach Roach started to call for another goalkeeper change.

He'd got as far as 'Whose turn–' before Hacker and Studs ≡***flew* off at record speed** and planted themselves as strikers in front of the goal, again.

'Looks like it's my turn,' I said. I put on the gloves, set myself up in goal, and **waited for the chaos to begin**!

And I didn't have long to wait! Ricardo and Nic were doing their best, but they were **totally worn-out** from all the running they'd done in the first half.

Of course Studs and Hacker didn't help at all, so I found myself facing non-stop, super-hard, super-close shots on goal. I was doing my best, but **I was taking a lot of hits**, and it was never-ending!

There was finally a break in play, and I called out to Studs and Hacker to take their turn in goal. At which point, **statue-Studs and statue-Hacker were back**! I knew they heard me, but they absolutely did not move one millimetre! It would have been pretty amazing, if it wasn't so annoying . . .

The game quickly restarted, so it looked like I was stuck in goal for the rest of the game. **And it didn't get any easier!**

The shots kept flying at me. **I made a lot of saves**—some of which I actually meant—and lots where the ball just hit random parts of my body and deflected away from goal. I kept nearly all of the shots out of the net . . . but **two or three did get through**.

At the end of the game, Studs and Hacker were quick to tell me that **they thought I should have made more saves**.

'I'm very disappointed with that goalkeeping performance, Tiny Timmy,' said Studs. '**Thanks for making us lose.** I can't believe some of those goals you let in!'

'Yeah,' said Hacker. 'Sometimes you've just got to put your body on the line.'

'Are you kidding!' I said. '**I made heaps of saves and got smashed all over**, just because you guys were too busy twiddling your thumbs up the other end of the court and not doing any defending at all! If it wasn't for me and Nic and Ricardo, **we'd have lost by twenty**!'

'Well, don't forget all the goals we scored to keep us in the game,' said Studs.

'One goal!' I said. 'And even that was a fluke!'

'Well, yes, one goal,' said Studs, 'but we can **put that down to poor service**. We would have scored heaps more if you'd actually passed us the ball.'

'Yeah,' said Hacker, 'we probably would have both scored hat tricks. At least.'

'Are they always like this?' asked Nic.

'Unfortunately, yes!' I said. Thankfully Sienna and Mike had come over to talk to us.

'We're really **sorry for taking so many shots**!' said Sienna.

'And we didn't mean for them to hit you so much!' said Mike. '**You just did too good a job**, getting in the way all the time!'

I laughed, and said, 'Hey, it's not your fault! **It's all just part of the game.** And the good news is there's only one more training session in here before we get to **play a real match outside** on the weekend!'

We couldn't wait!

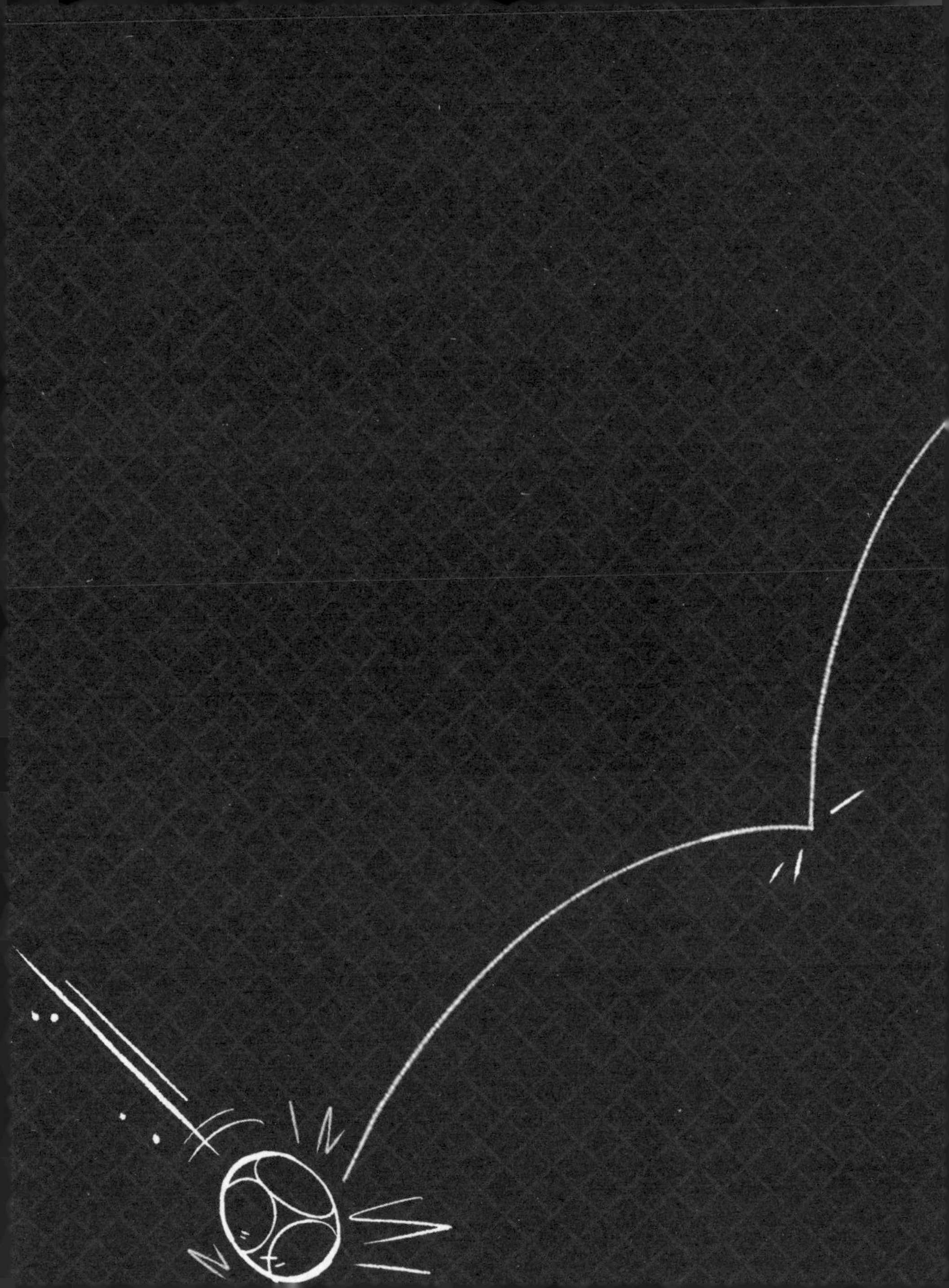

CHAPTER 6

The next morning was rough! If I thought I felt sore the day after our first indoor training session, then how I was feeling now was at **a whole other level**! And Nic wasn't feeling much better!

We'd both been hit in pretty much every part of our bodies when we'd been trying to make saves yesterday. We'd taken **so long to walk to school** that we only just made it through the gates before the bell rang!

I'd had muscle aches and strains before, and even some bruises and scrapes. But getting in the way of hard-hit shots was **a different kind of hurt**—and I'd had to do it for a whole half at training yesterday. I was glad I wasn't a full-time goalkeeper, like Liam!

Not unexpectedly, **I didn't get a lot of sympathy** from Studs and Hacker . . .

'Can you believe this guy, Hacker?' said Studs. 'Shuffling and shambling around **like he's a hundred years old**.'

'Yeah,' said Hacker. 'He's definitely making the most of it.'

'Anyway,' Studs went on, '**aren't goalkeepers supposed to use their hands**? If you'd just done that we wouldn't have had to listen to you complaining all day.'

'First,' I said, 'I haven't complained for one second to anyone! And second, I wouldn't have been hit in the body so much if you guys **had actually done some defending**.'

Studs started to go on about being a striker who didn't have to defend, but I jumped in again. 'And third, it's not so easy to make saves only with your hands–**perhaps you'll find that out** when you actually take your turn in goal.'

'Unlikely,' said Studs. 'Coach Roach **won't make us play goalkeeper**. He knows how valuable we are as strikers.'

'Yeah,' said Hacker. 'Coach and us, **we have . . . an arrangement**.'

'Sure,' I said, shaking my head. It was time for training, so I guessed we'd find out soon enough!

Coach Roach started the session with **some quick passing drills**, to help get our touch right. We began by all standing in a big circle, passing the ball to the other side with just one kick each.

Then we broke into groups and did a pass-and-shoot drill. This was good for getting us to **pass, move and shoot, all with one touch**.

We started on the half-way line by passing the ball to a teammate who was standing out on the sideline. They passed the ball back, with one touch, and after moving forward the first player took a first-time shot.

This was trickier than it sounded, because everything had to be smooth for it to work, **with every touch perfect**!

Then, even if we got the first part right, we had to shoot the ball past Liam. He had hardly had to make a save yesterday in the training match, so **he was super fresh and hard to beat**!

It took a bit of practice, but soon we were getting shots on target, and even scoring some goals! We all thought this was a really good drill to help us use the ball in a small space and a short time. Perfect for futsal!

We finished up that drill, and Coach Roach gathered everyone around.

'Alright,' Coach said, 'we'll be playing another practice match in a moment. Same teams as last time.'

Ricardo, Nic and I all groaned.

'What's the problem, Tiny Timmy?' said Studs. 'All you guys have to do is make more saves and pass the ball to us every time you get it. Then we'll do the rest.'

'Easy,' added Hacker.

Coach Roach continued, 'Now listen up, **LIONS**. With this being our last session before our game on the weekend, I want everyone to take this practice match as seriously as possible. Which means, **no nonsense**.'

'Absolutely, Coach,' said Studs. 'I'm glad you mentioned that. Hacker and I were discussing only this morning that some unnamed members of our team haven't been putting in a serious effort with their goalkeeping and defending.' Studs was **nodding his head in our direction** as he said all this.

'Yeah,' said Hacker. 'And the service to the strikers has been **practically non-existent**.'

'Hmmm,' murmured Coach Roach. **'That's not quite the way I saw it.'**

'Oh,' said Studs. 'How did you see it, Coach? Worse even than I thought?' He nodded across at us again.

'Actually,' Coach Roach said, 'what stood out most was two players playing out of position and **not taking their turn at being goalkeeper**.'

'Really?!' said Studs. 'That is bad. But **whoever could you mean**?' He and Hacker slowly scanned the squad. 'I don't see them, Coach. Perhaps you should unveil the culprits now.'

Coach Roach eyed Studs and Hacker. **'I'm looking at them,'** he said.

'What's that, Coach?' asked Studs. **'Surely you can't mean . . . us?!'** Studs staggered back in shock.

'Yeah,' said Hacker. 'What happened to our arrangement?!'

'Sorry lads, but there was never any arrangement,' said Coach Roach. 'And to make up for yesterday's session, today **you will definitely take your turn in goal**. For a whole half. Each.'

This time both Studs and Hacker practically collapsed. **'This can't be!'** said Studs. 'You know as well as we do that as natural strikers, it's in the team's best interests for us to stay up front scoring goals!'

'Yeah,' said Hacker. 'What you're suggesting is **against the laws of nature**!'

Coach wasn't impressed. 'Let's not forget that you're both in the team as defenders. And that you did no defending at all yesterday. And apart from that, **it's only fair for everyone to have a turn** playing goalkeeper—just like your teammates did.'

Studs and Hacker weren't happy, but they didn't have a choice. And I was . . . **super excited**!

With Ricardo, Nic and I all playing on the court, it looked like **we might actually be able to compete** with the other team this time!

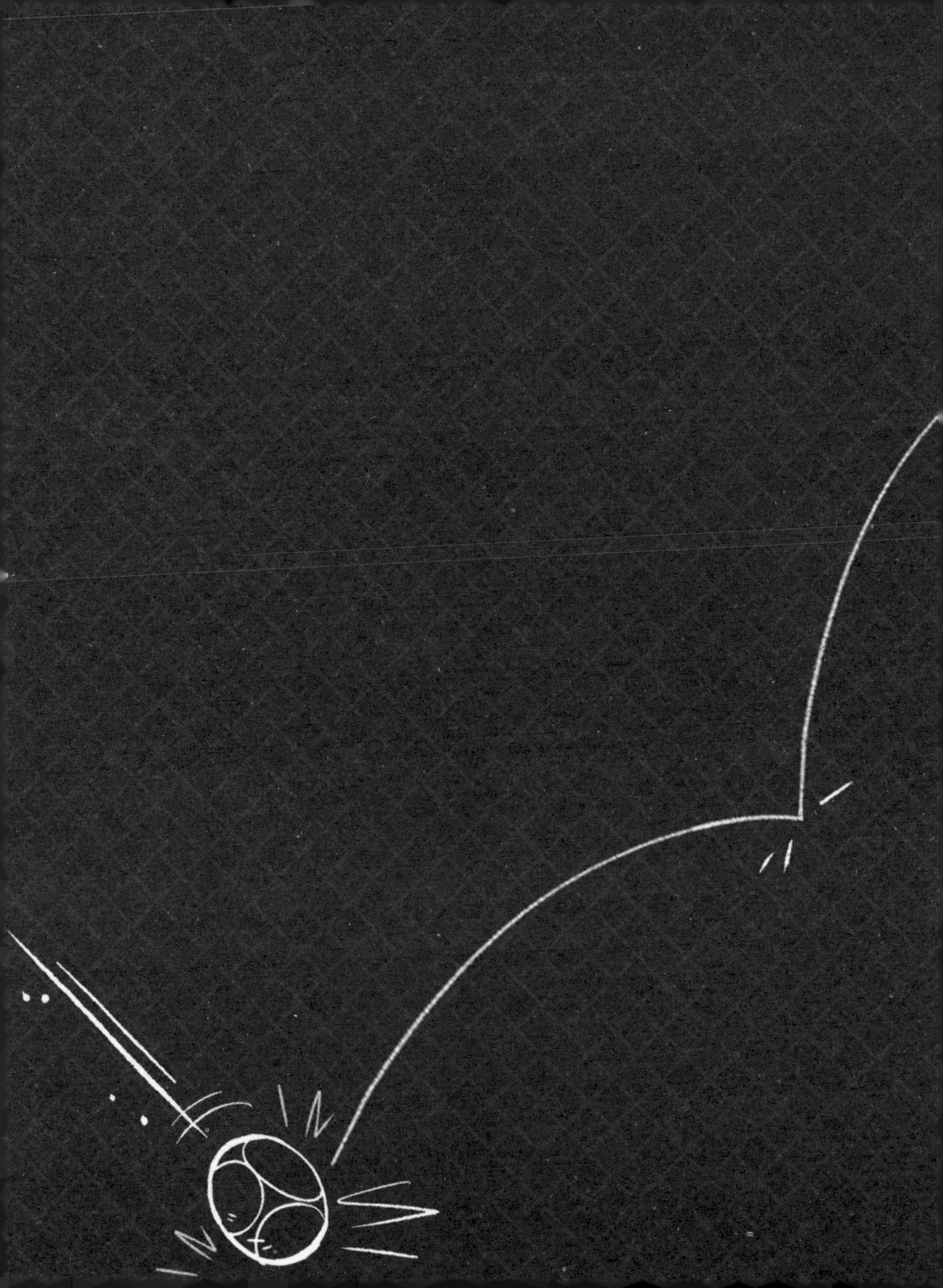

CHAPTER 7

It didn't take long for us to see what a difference it made with our rejigged team! We all had an extra spring in our step, and the game was already so much more fun to play than the one we played yesterday!

With Studs in goal for the first half, Nic, Ricardo and I were able to do a much better job of defending Sienna, Mike and Millie. Even Hacker stayed back to defend! It was like we were finally playing like **a proper team**!

And with our defence a lot more solid, we were able to **put some really good moves together in attack, too**! We played lots of one-touch passes, kept moving into space, and really **concentrated on our ball control**.

The other team didn't know what had hit them! For the first time they actually had to do some proper defending against us. I didn't say it out loud, but it was good to see them having to do **some huffing and puffing for a change**!

We scored some amazing goals, too, with some great passing moves. Finally, with some helpful teammates, it felt like I was **really getting the hang of this futsal thing**!

We did have **a bit of trouble** down the other end, though.

It wasn't super surprising, but it turned out Studs hadn't been in a great position to criticise our goalkeeping. He was excellent at doing over-the-top, fancy-looking dives, but there was just one problem.

He kept missing the ball!

Shots went over his arms,

under his arms–

one even went straight through his legs!

We thought that was bad, but that was nothing compared to Hacker when he had his turn in goal in the second half.

Because it turned out Hacker was . . . **scared of the ball**! Which is definitely not a good quality for a goalkeeper to have. Every time a shot came in, instead of trying to save it, **Hacker jumped out of the way**!

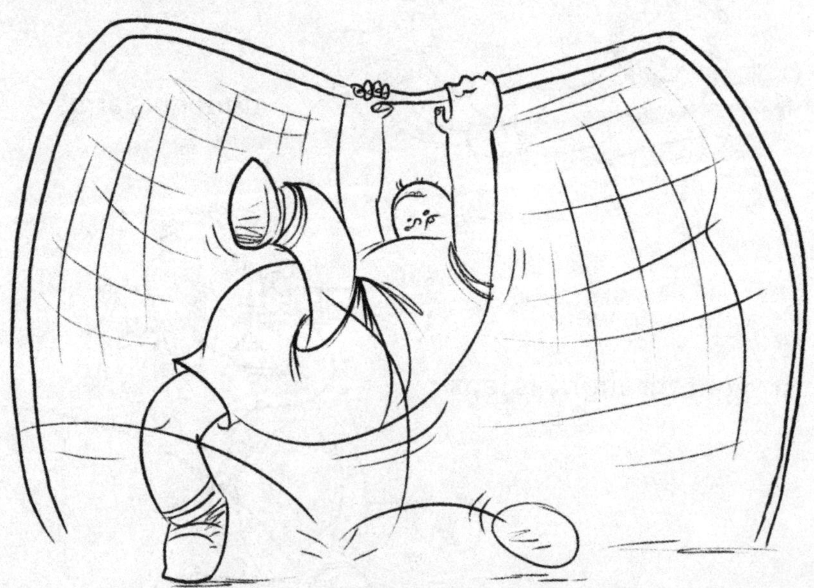

It was lucky we scored a lot of goals of our own, because between them Studs and Hacker let in a bunch for the other team. It was close, but **we ended up winning the game**!

'What was going on there?!' I said to Hacker and Studs, as we walked to the bench. 'We almost lost because of that crazy goalkeeping!'

For once, Studs and Hacker didn't have much to say!

'Ah, just a bad day, I guess,' said Studs.

'Yeah,' said Hacker. 'I'd prefer not to comment at this time.'

I could have gone back to them with all the stuff they'd said yesterday about how goalkeepers were supposed to use their hands—but to be honest I was just **grateful for the peace and quiet**!

All in all, I was feeling much better after our session today. Even the bruises and scrapes didn't seem to hurt as much! And best of all, with all our training out of the way, I could **really look forward to the weekend** and an actual game of outdoor soccer!

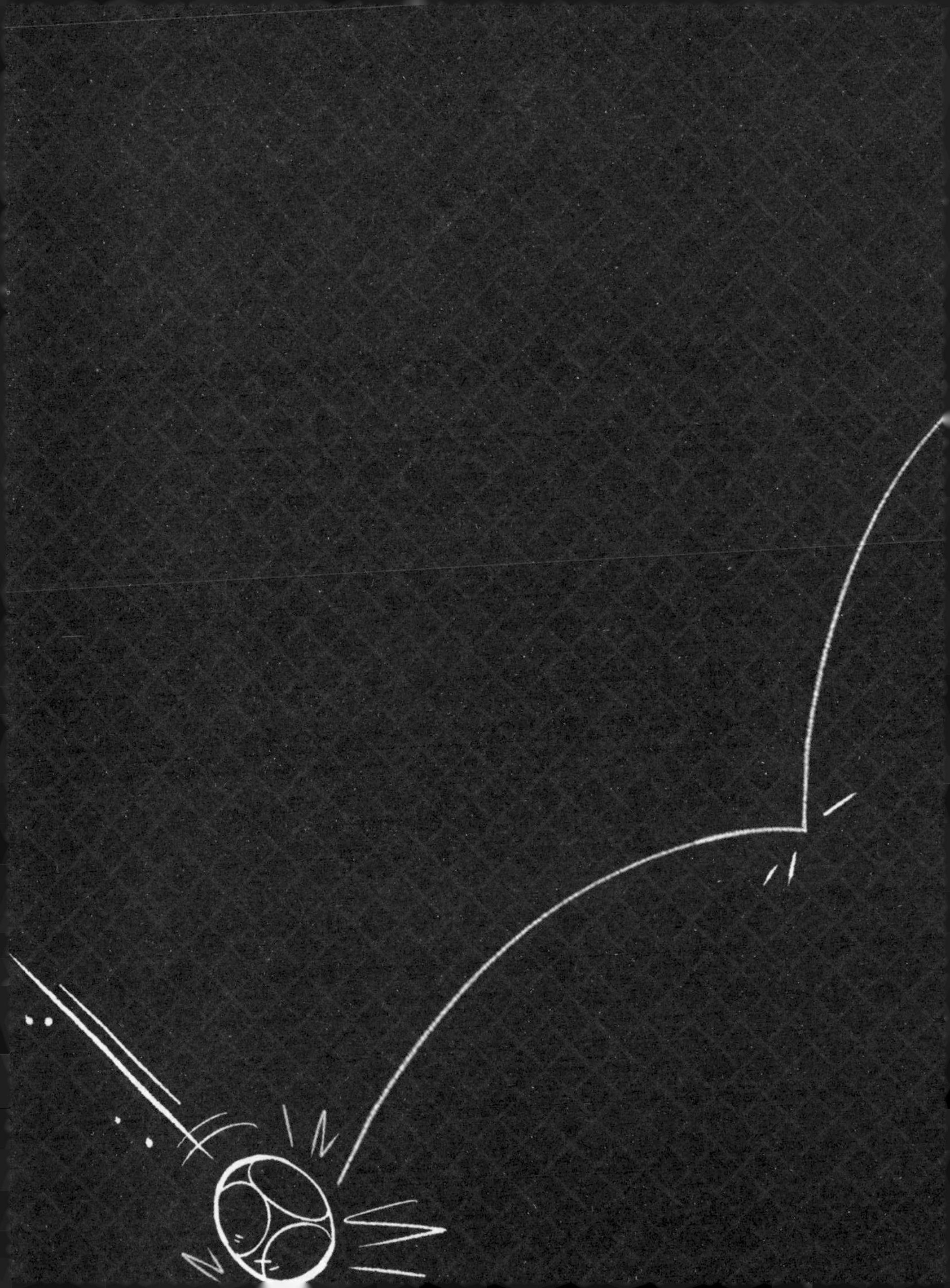

By the morning of the game, I was feeling absolutely amazing! The aches and pains were gone, and I was ready to go!

Nic had got over his bumps and bruises, too. He **couldn't wait to get out on the full-size field** for the first time!

This was the first of our away games before our home pitch was ready for us to play on again. It took us

a while to get to the oval, but when we got there, **I could see Nic's face light up**!

And I was excited as well! We ran onto the pitch—it seemed like there was so much space out there after our week of training indoors! I was so happy for Nic to finally be able to play on a proper, full-size, grass pitch!

We had a surprise for Nic, too. Coach Roach called everybody in for our pre-match team talk, and asked Nic to come up to the front.

'Nic, we've really enjoyed having you with us for the past week,' Coach said. 'You've trained fantastically well, and it seems like **you've been a part of the team forever**.'

Nic gave a big, beaming smile. 'Thanks, Coach,' he said. 'I've had a great time!'

'Well,' Coach said, 'as a full member of the team, you're going to need this.' Coach took out a **LIONS** shirt and presented it to Nic. Everyone clapped and **gave Nic a big cheer**!

Nic looked so proud! He pulled the shirt on, and we listened while Coach gave the rest of his team talk. As he finished up, the ref blew the whistle for the teams to run out onto the pitch. **It was go time!**

Straight from the kick-off we could see how much our indoor training had helped. We'd got so used to being able to control the ball in tight spaces and play one-touch passes that it seemed like **we could do anything we wanted**! The other team had no chance!

We were able to keep the ball almost non-stop, moving it around and controlling the game. And when you can do that, one thing usually happens—your team scores goals. And we did! **We were three-nil up by half time!**

Our very best goal, though, came in the second half. We used **the skills we'd learned from all the drills** we'd worked on in the hall!

First, Ricardo won the ball and went off on a mazy run through a bunch of the other team's players. Just like **the dribbling drill** we'd done through the cones in our first training session!

Ricardo passed the ball to Millie, who hit a first-time pass to Mike, who then passed it straight back to Ricardo, who had continued his run. Just like **the one-touch drill** we'd done at training!

Ricardo looked up and played a long ball my way. I had defenders around me on every side, but I managed to control the ball on my chest and bring it down. **Coach Roach's 'boxed in' drill** had been perfect practice!

I played the ball back to Nic, who was in some space, but had a defender directly in front. He passed it out to Sienna, who was set up out wide, and she sent

it straight back to Nic, who had run past the defender. Nic hit a first-time shot at goal, and . . . it went zooming past the keeper, into the top corner! **The pass-and-shoot drill** had worked perfectly!

Which meant **Nic had scored in his first game as a LION**! And what a goal it was! We could see Coach Roach on the sideline with his arms in the air, cheering–and no wonder! All the things we'd worked so hard on at training had paid off!

We ended up winning the match 5-0, and it was as **close to a perfect game** as we'd ever played! And a lot of it was down to our indoor training. We still had a few more weeks of that to go, and even after all the bumps and bruises we'd taken, we were excited to keep up our training in the school hall.

Sienna said we should start a team in the futsal comp at the local indoor centre. We all agreed it would be **just the right way to improve our skills** in the off-season. I only had one condition . . .

'We need to get Liam to play,' I said. 'I don't think I can take a whole season playing in goal!'

'That's for sure,' said Ricardo, and everyone else agreed!

That was something for us to look forward to. Right now, **we were excited that Nic was going to be with us** for a whole term!

'How did it feel out there?' I asked Nic. 'One goal from one game—pretty great strike rate!'

'It was the best!' Nic replied. 'I can't wait to play some more games on full-size fields!'

'And just wait till our home ground is ready for us to play on!' said Sienna. 'It's going to be like playing on a professional pitch!'

We were all super excited for that, and we knew that Nic was going to make a huge difference to our team. This week had sure had its ups and downs, but right now it looked like **the only way was up**!

COLLECT THEM ALL!

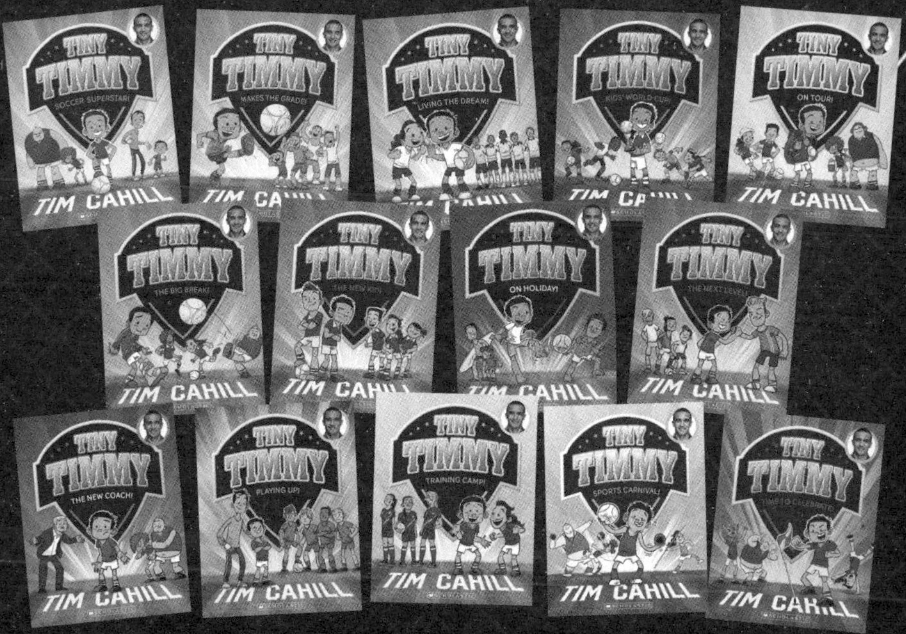

Look out for more

TINY TIMMY

books coming soon!

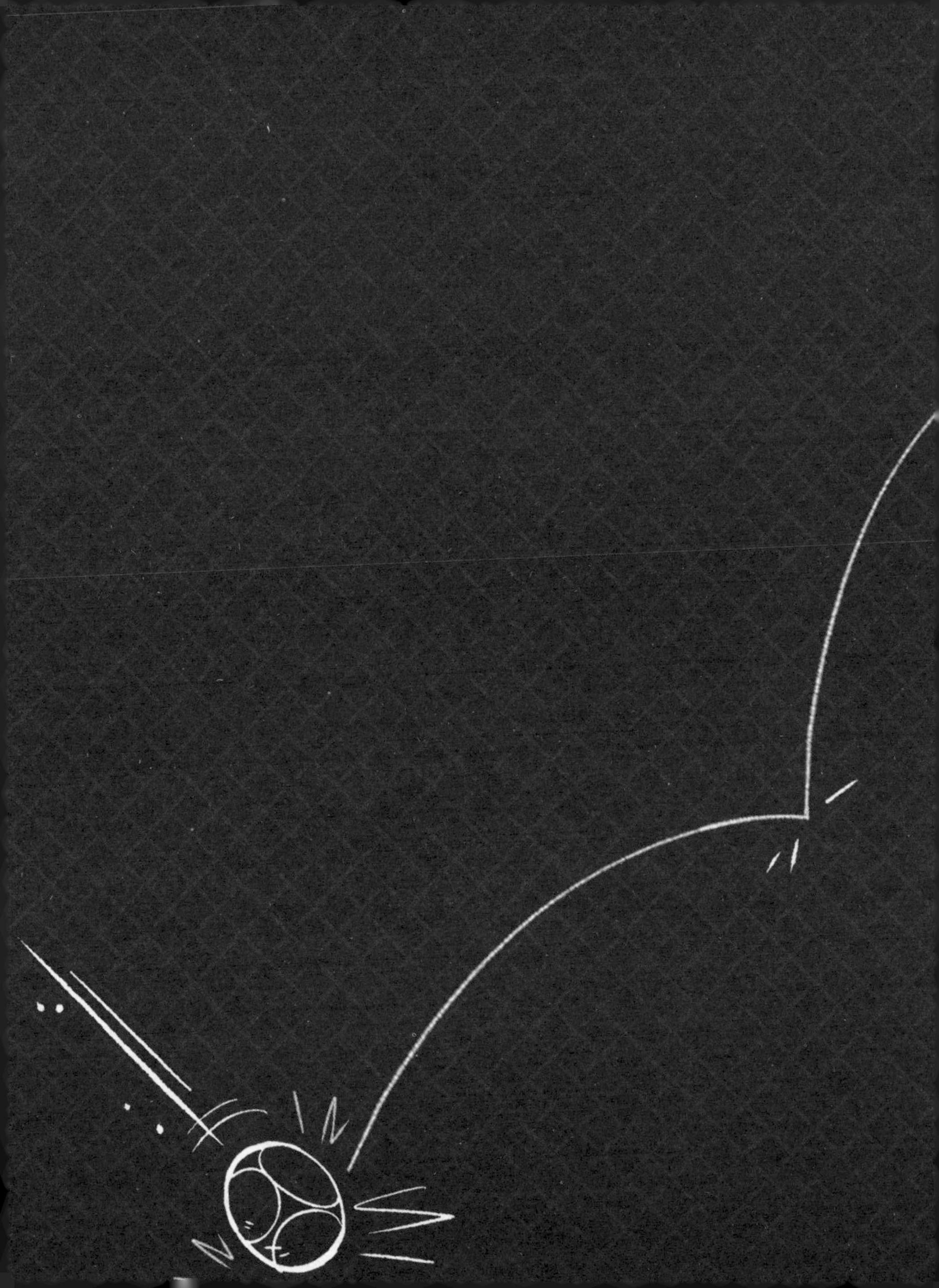